Fat Cat of Underwhere
Text copyright © 2009 by Bruce Hale
Illustrations copyright © 2009 by Shane Hillman
All rights reserved. Printed in the United States of America.

Library of Congress Cataloging-in-Publication Data
Hale, Bruce.
  Fat cat of Underwhere / by Bruce Hale ; illustrated by Shane Hillman.
— 1st ed.
    p. cm. — (Underwhere ; #4)
  Summary: Dodging government spies and three-horned beasties, Fitz
the cat and his human friends, Stephanie, Zeke, and Hector, venture once
more into the mysterious land of Underwhere to recover the magical
scepter, which looks suspiciously like a bejewelled toilet plunger.
  ISBN 978-0-06-085133-0 (trade bdg. : alk. paper)
  [1. Adventure and adventurers—Fiction. 2. Heroes—Fiction. 3. Magic—
Fiction. 4. Cats—Fiction. 5. Humorous stories.] I. Hillman, Shane, ill. II. Title.
PZ7.H1295Fat 2009   2008031476
[Fic]—dc22   CIP
                                                                       AC

Typography by Jennifer Heuer
09 10 11 12 13 LP/RRDB 10 9 8 7 6 5 4 3 2 1
❖
First Edition

FAT CAT UNDERW

by BRUCE HALL

illustrated by
SHANE HILLMAN

HARPER

An Imprint of HarperCollins*Publishers*

To
Mom and Lee,
Cat Ladies
with class

Trouble with Garlic and Onion

Let's face it, humans are pretty hopeless. I don't know how you make it through this world.

You can barely hear or see. You have no claws or fangs to speak of. You can't smell (although you *do* smell, if you catch my drift). And worst of all, where your glorious tail should wave, you don't even have a stump to wiggle.

In fact, if you didn't feed us, pet us, and scratch us in that special place under the chin, I'd be half tempted to write you off altogether.

So imagine my disgust and surprise when I found myself turning *human*.

No, not physically (perish the thought!). But *mentally*.

One day I'm looking out for Number One, being fabulously selfish, the way cats should be. The next day I'm attacking evil magicians and helping children save the world.

It's not *natural*. It's not *right*.

I blame it all on that wicked little man who smells like rotten eggs.

Shortly after the neighbor children, Zeke and Stephanie, got this fancy old litter bowl (*toilet*, I believe you humans call it), Rotten Egg Man started showing up. Trouble followed. And bit by bit, I began talking and acting more like a human than a proper cat.

Don't believe me? How else can you explain this latest episode in my entanglement with Underwhere (the place, not those ridiculous things humans wear under their clothes)?

One fine day in spring, I was leaping up and down outside a classroom window. (Is *that* any way for a cat to behave, I ask you?)

My human, Hector, was inside, doing whatever humans do at their school. And I urgently needed to tell him something.

But schools are not built with cats in mind. Cat paws, though clever, cannot open doorknobs. So I jumped up and down like a nincompoop (or a dog—same thing) to catch his eye.

Finally, the boy spotted me and hurried out.

"Fitz?" he said. "What are *you* doing here?"

"Acting like a mouse-brained dunce," I said. "Listen, there's trouble back home."

Hector just shook his head. "You know I can't understand you up here."

I rolled my eyes. Fur balls and fish bones! *I* can understand humans, but *they* can't understand me unless we're in Underwhere, that strange land

3

below our world.

So, I trotted a little way toward the school gate and looked back over my shoulder.

"What is it?" said Hector.

I repeated the move.

"You want me to go with you?" he asked.

That's my Hector—slow on the uptake, but he gets it eventually.

I nodded.

"Sorry, Fitzie," he said. "I can't leave school yet."

"Oh, for the love of mice," I muttered, trotting back to Hector. I bit his pants leg and tugged.

"All right, all right," he said. "I'll try to get off. But this better be important."

Hector hurried inside. A minute later, he rejoined me.

I led the way as we hustled back to my territory—otherwise known as the Center of the

Universe. In front of the neighbors' house, a stinky metal box on wheels (*car,* I believe you humans call it) was waiting. In it sat a big-eyed old man who smelled like mothballs.

"By Aphrodite's nightie!" he cried. "Thank heavens you've come!"

"Dr. Prufrock!" said Hector, approaching the car. "What's wrong?"

"It's the, er, Scepter," the old man whispered. "We must hide it someplace safe."

Hector's eyes brightened. "You *found* the Scepter?"

"Shh!" said the old man. Fear scent rolled off of him, stronger than Hector's grandmother's cheap perfume. If he'd had a tail, it would've been curled between his legs.

"I brought the Scepter here," he said, "thinking we could figure out something together. When I found you children weren't home, I tried to leave.

But my car wouldn't start."

"Let's see it," said Hector.

Mothball Man picked up a cloth-covered item. He unwrapped it.

My human took the object, a short stick with a bell-shaped thingie attached. "Where did you find it?" he asked. He held it up, and pretty rocks on its shaft twinkled in the sunlight. Supernatural power pulsed from it, making my whiskers quiver.

"Careful!" said Prufrock. "Keep it hidden. The Scepter mustn't fall into the wrong—"

Screeech!

Just then, a car pulled in behind us. Two men in dark suits, dark hats, and huge pink sunglasses stared from it intently.

Well, tug my tail! It was the government spies the kids called Agent Belly and Agent Mole. (To my mind, they were Onion Breath and Garlic Breath.)

"What's that?" called Garlic Breath.

"Looks like a magical object," said Onion Breath.

For *some* reason, these two were eager to get their paws on some magic. I guess without cat powers, humans have to make do as best they can.

Mothball Man shrank back into his car. Up went the window.

Hector turned to face the men and slipped the Scepter behind his back. "What, this?" he said. "Just a bathroom plunger. Nothing special."

The two spies climbed out of their car.

"If it's nothing special, then you won't mind us having a look," said Onion Breath, waddling over. His onion stench made my nostrils flinch.

Hector backed up. "But it's all dirty. You might catch something."

"Had it already," said Garlic Breath, extending his hand.

My boy shot a glance at Mothball Man, who had slid so low in his seat only his eyes and white hair showed. No help *there*.

Hector kept backing away from the two men in black.

"Over here!" I called from behind them.

Hector spotted me. He hefted the Scepter and tossed it over the heads of the spies.

"Hey!" cried Onion Breath.

I snatched up the object in my jaws. *Oof*, it was heavy. Cats aren't meant to fetch and carry. (Others fetch *for* us—it's only right.)

I carried the Scepter off, but it slowed me down.

"Here, kitty!" called Garlic Breath, closing in.

My neck and jaw were straining. Too much weight . . .

The Scepter slipped from my mouth and hit the ground—*tonk!*

"Nice pussykins," said Onion Breath. *He* was anything *but* nice.

Behind the men, Hector shouted, "Stay away from my cat!"

"Easy now," said Garlic Breath.

I growled. My magnificent tail lashed the air.

The two men pulled on thick black gloves and advanced cautiously, hands held out. They'd *better* be cautious. They were taking on a backyard tiger.

And this tiger was ready to rumble.

Dino Dog

Whoosh!

From nowhere, a figure shot through the space between us. It scooped up the Scepter, leaving behind a scent of . . . pizza?

"Zeke!" cried Hector.

It was the neighbor kid, Hector's friend. Obnoxious, rude, and a real yank on the tail, he was also quick on his feet.

"Hand it over!" cried Onion Breath. "Your government commands you!"

"Oh, really?" came another voice. "Where's your letter from the president to prove it?"

Zeke's sister, Stephanie, marched up, smelling like spring in a pine forest.

"None of your business," Onion Breath said. "Give us that toilet plunger. Now!"

He reached for Zeke.

The boy danced sideways and tossed the Scepter to Hector. "*I* don't have it."

Garlic Breath snarled, "Give it!" He strode toward my human.

Hector threw the object to Stephanie. "*I* don't have it."

"Children," Onion Breath snapped. "This isn't a game."

But in fact it was. And the spies were losing.

"*Grrr!*" Garlic growled as he whirled on the girl.

"Over here!" I called.

Even though she couldn't understand my words, Steph threw me the Scepter. (She *is* the smartest of the bunch.)

But she hadn't counted on Garlic Breath. The tall spy stretched out his arms, and the Scepter bounced off his hand into the bushes.

"Oh, no!" cried Stephanie. Her hands flew to her face, and the smell of worry rolled off her like thick cigar smoke.

Garlic Breath bent and pawed through the shrubbery.

Zeke and Hector leaped forward.

"Enough!" said Onion Breath, patting a bulge in his jacket. (I smelled oiled metal.)

The other spy gave a triumphant cry. He reached and tugged. Then his face collapsed into a frown as something tugged back.

"Eh?"

A strong, funky odor hit my nostrils—a blend of dog and . . . lizard?

"What th—?" said Garlic Breath. My thoughts exactly.

All the hairs on my back stood up as a strange creature exploded from the bushes. It combined the ugliness of a dog with the scariness of a giant lizard. Three horns jutted from its broad head. A powerful black-furred body tapered into a scaly tail.

It carried the Scepter in its jaws, and it was headed straight at me!

"Reeeow!"

Every backyard tiger knows there's a time to fight and a time to run. *This* was the time to run.

I shot across the driveway and up the nearest tree.

"Gurrrumph!" the creature growled around the stick in its mouth.

I clung to the lowest branch and looked down.

The humans screamed and scampered about. If they'd had a little cat sense, they would have joined me.

"Don't let it escape!" cried Onion Breath. He

chased the dog-lizard thing, but when it whirled on him, he screamed and fled. *"Aaugh!"*

"It's got the Scepter!" Stephanie shouted. "Stop it!"

Zeke leaped aside as the creature thundered past. *"You* stop it."

Hector crouched, ready to catch the monster. At the last second, the dog-lizard feinted with its horns, and Hector hopped back, landing on his butt in the bushes.

From my perch, I watched the thing power down the sidewalk and push through the fence around a half-built house.

"Don't look now, but it's going into the construction site," I said.

Zeke glanced down the street. "Hey, you guys, it's going into the construction site."

My whiskers twitched. "My, aren't you the clever one."

The boy ignored me.

"Let's go!" cried Stephanie.

The spies seized her and Zeke. "Not so fast," said Onion Breath.

"But, the monster—" said Zeke, struggling.

"Exactly," said Garlic Breath.

Onion Breath loomed over the kids. "Where did you get that thing?"

"Us?" said Stephanie. "It's not *our* doggie-lizard-whatever."

"Likely story," said Garlic Breath.

"She's right," said Zeke. "We don't even know what it is."

My human frowned. "Let's see, it had the head of a triceratops, the body of a Labrador retriever, and the fur of a poodle," he said. "That makes it . . ."

"A labceradle?" said Stephanie.

"A poobradoratops?" said Zeke.

"Nope," said Hector. "A . . . triceradoodle."

I shifted on the branch. "Whatever you call it, it's going to Underwhere."

Everybody ignored me. Tch, *humans*.

Onion Breath growled. "You children had better bring back that tricera-whatsit, and the magical thingamajig, too."

"That's what we're *trying* to do," said Stephanie.

"If you'll just let us go," said Zeke.

The two spies looked at each other.

"All right," said Onion Breath. "But if you try to pull a fast one . . ."

"Us?" said Hector. "Never."

In his case, *never* meant not in the last five minutes.

Nevertheless, the spies let go, and the children started off.

"Wait," said Hector.

"What?" said Zeke.

My human pointed up at me. "Fitz. We need

him to track the Triceradoodle."

"Hector's right," said Stephanie. "It's got a head start."

They gazed up at me. I pretended not to notice and busied myself with cleaning my paws. (Tree climbing is *filthy* work.)

"What do you say, Fitzie?" said Hector.

I shook my head.

"Please?" said Stephanie. "We'll give you a nice piece of tuna for dinner."

My tail twitched. We needed the Scepter, but it would take a lot more than tuna to make *this* cat chase a savage dino dog.

"And that electric blanket you wanted?" said Hector. "All yours."

Aw, wax my whiskers.

I knew I would regret it. I sighed a long sigh—twice the usual length, for maximum effect—and climbed down from the tree. Then I led the way

17

to the half-built house where the portal to Under-where waited.

A *normal* cat would've stayed up in the tree.

I was well past being a normal cat.

Cat's Best Friend

Not only did those ungrateful humans refuse to carry me on the long walk home, but they also gave me dry cat food for dinner.

What sort of meal is that for a Mighty Kittykins? I ask you.

When the humans had finished their own meal (no dry food there), we gathered in the great room of Stephanie and Zeke's house.

Stephanie had spread open a rotten-egg-smelling paper thingie (*book*, I believe you humans call it) on the table. I sat on her lap for maximum petting, and the boys crowded close.

Zeke flipped a page. "Does it say how to get into the cave?"

"Careful," said Stephanie, elbowing him. "*The Book of Booty* is ancient."

I gazed at the book. Although I can understand spoken human language, I can't read it. Everything looked like worm wriggles on a sidewalk.

"*Bo-*ring," I said. As usual, they ignored me.

Stephanie pointed. "This is interesting . . ."

I nudged her arm. She petted me as she read aloud:

> "*Where three-horned beastie lies awake*
> *And hoards the prize across the lake,*
> *Beware the wee folk, fierce and fuzzy,*
> *And trick them, though their tails be*
>   *skuzzy—*"

Fish bones and fur balls. I hate poetry.

In one fluid move, I leaped from her lap onto the open book. "It's *simple*," I said. "We borrow a boat, paddle out, distract the lizard-doggie, steal the Scepter, and defeat Rotten Egg Man. Then I can finally get back to normal."

Blank looks greeted me.

"Do you mind?" said Hector, lifting me aside. "We're trying to read."

I rolled my eyes. Books wouldn't solve our problem. No matter. Dark time is hunting time. And I was still enough of a cat to know that.

"See you kitties later," I drawled. "The night is calling."

I trotted across the room, into their kitchen, and out through the cat door. (One of the top-five best human inventions, along with the can opener.)

At the top of the steps I groomed myself. No sense going out on the town looking shabby.

I sniffed the cool night air. On it floated the news of the neighborhood: people, pork chops, jasmine blossoms, the funk of a dog from two yards down, and the stink of a car engine.

Poor humans, with your puny noses. You don't know what you're missing.

I sauntered down the steps and around the house. Long grass tickled my belly. An owl hooted.

Then, under the car stench, I picked up a new scent: Mouse! I froze. With eyes, nose, and ears I scanned the front yard.

There! Twenty tail lengths ahead, the grass twitched. *Mmm.* A nice, juicy mouse would erase that dry-cat-food taste.

Slowly, I stalked forward, eyes on the prize. I was a ghost, a whisper, a rumor. Mousie wouldn't even know what hit her.

Ten tail lengths away, I froze again.

The car's metal-and-oil stink was even stronger, and I could hear two humans sitting inside the big steel box, yakking.

"What are they talking about now?" said a smooth voice.

"Books," the rougher voice growled.

The voices seemed familiar.

The wind shifted, and I caught their scent. It was Garlic Breath and Onion Breath, the two spies. But why were they sitting in a darkened car, listening to the children?

"*Books?*" Smooth Voice said. "You're using that fancy gizmo to listen to kids doing *homework?* Let *me* try."

"Uh-uh," said Rough Voice. "My turn."

Grass rustled. My mouse snack was on the move.

I sank into a hunter's crouch, tail twitching.

Come to Papa, mousie.

"No way," Onion Breath whined. "You *always* get to use the cool gadgets; I never do."

"Chief said," growled Garlic Breath.

"She always liked you best." Onion Breath sounded sulky. "Fine. Then, I'll use the scope, see if I can spot any magical doodads."

Uh-oh.

We had two power objects at the house. If the spies took them, I might *never* get back to normal.

While I hesitated, a blur of wings beat the air. A huge owl swooped down and snatched the mouse from under my nose.

Aw, sparrow guts! Served me right for thinking like a human.

I snarled. Silently I cursed the big feather head, the Triceradoodle, the spies, and the whole situation.

Enough. Like a shadow, I oozed behind a tree trunk.

"Now, where is that night scope?" Onion Breath muttered. Clatters and rustles came from the car.

I looked around. Somehow I had to distract these spies. But how?

The funky dog scent teased my nose again, and I smiled. When you need a ruckus, count on a Fido.

This particular Fido, named Vinnie, was sleeping in his yard two houses down.

But not for long.

I zipped along the line of bushes and leaped onto his fence. Carefully I nudged open the gate latch to make things easier for the poor, dumb doggie.

"Hey, Vinnie!" I called.

No response. The mutt snored on.

"Hey, Alpo brains!" I yowled.

Still no answer.

When in doubt, go back to basics. I hopped off the fence, trotted up to ol' Vinnie, and batted his big, ugly nose.

"*Wrrroof!*" The shaggy monster bolted to his feet, half awake.

"You big bag of dumbness," I said. "You couldn't find your tail if it was sticking out of your mouth."

Finally, Vinnie got the picture. "Cat!" he barked. "Cat, cat!"

I dashed across the yard and up onto the fence. "Is *that* the best you got? Come and get me, you great tub of puppy chow!"

Vinnie's paws scrabbled in the dirt, and he launched himself in pursuit.

I jumped down onto the sidewalk.

Bam! The gate blew open behind me.

I glanced back. *Holy whiskers*, he was fast.

"Cat! Bad cat!" barked Vinnie.

Tearing down the sidewalk, I reached the spies' car just as Onion Breath leaned out the window.

"Coming through!" I cried. And I sprang to the car's windowsill, scrambling up Onion Breath's face to the roof.

"Hey!" he said.

In hot pursuit, Vinnie flung himself at the car door, smack into the spy.

"Aaugh!" cried Onion Breath.

"Roof, roof!" barked Vinnie. "Cat on roof!"

The spy swatted at the big, hairy bruiser. "Down, you mutt!"

I sat on the roof and began cleaning my fur. Neatness counts, after all.

Over and over, Vinnie threw himself at the car, barking madly. The noise drew his owner to her front door. "Vinnie! Here, boy!" a woman called.

Zeke and Stephanie's front door swung open too. "What's going on out here?" called Caitlyn, their older cousin.

"Whoops," said Garlic Breath.

"Time to go," said Onion Breath.

"Roof, roof, roof!" barked Vinnie.

The car engine roared. I gathered myself and eyed the nearby tree. It would be a tricky one.

Shhcreee! The car rocketed into motion. As it passed the tree, I leaped through space—right over Vinnie's surprised muzzle—and onto the trunk.

"*Oof!*" My landing knocked all the wind out of me. Weakly I scootched a little higher, until I was out of the dog's reach.

"Tree, tree!" barked Vinnie. "Cat in tree!"

And there I clung, until Caitlyn and the kids came to rescue me.

Movie Magic

I'd be lying if I said I didn't enjoy all the fuss that followed. Caitlyn and Stephanie petted me, cooed over me, and gave me milk. Hector cuddled me and scratched my favorite spot. Even Zeke was less obnoxious than usual.

Not that that's saying much.

After everything had settled down, Caitlyn announced a special treat. "Listen up, you dorgwollops. I just heard that there's, like, a movie shooting here in town—directed by some German guy, Lars Von Breif. How's that for randomly cool?"

I understand human talk. But Caitlyn talk is a

whole other matter.

Hector smiled. "That's . . . random and cool."

"So, we are going to pile into the old four-wheel, motor. over there right now, and watch the movie magic." Caitlyn patted my head. "You too, Meow Mix."

"But—" Zeke began.

"Don't bother thanking me, Dinky Doodle. It's all done from a deep, deep well of cousinly love."

I licked my paw. Caitlyn has about as much love for Zeke as I have for the birds I torment.

"But we've got work to do," said Steph.

Caitlyn waved a hand. "Don't pop a gasket, Junie B. Brain. Your homework won't, like, turn rancid while we're gone."

"But really—" said Hector.

Caitlyn's eyes narrowed. "Maybe you zimwats didn't understand me. We. Are. Going. *Now!*"

And with that, she scooped me up and hustled

the kids into her little red car.

Ten minutes later, my ears were ringing from Caitlyn's nonstop monologue about boys, college classes, boys, her favorite movies, boys, greenhouse gases, and—oh yeah—boys. For the love of mice, that girl can talk!

I almost wished for a human's limited powers of hearing.

At last we drove through a gate and parked by some other cars in a wide field. The moon paled beside the blinding lights the humans had set up. Beyond several huge metal boxes on wheels, a crowd of people had gathered to watch something under the lights.

Hector pointed to a long, sardine-shaped tube with fins on a high platform. "Cool!" he cried. "A rocket ship!"

As we left the parking area, Caitlyn rushed over to a girl in green and revved up her mouth even more. The kids fidgeted.

Then a black bike pulled up. On it sat a big, blond lump who smelled like beans and corn chips and unwashed armpits.

"Hey, losers," said B.O. Boy.

"Melvin!" Zeke gasped, his face turning white.

The bully smiled like a dog flashing its canines. "Don't think I've forgotten how you tricked me into getting detention."

Hector, Stephanie, and Zeke looked at each other. "We, uh . . ." Zeke began.

"Just wanted you to know," said Melvin, "I'm a free man tomorrow."

Hector gulped. "You are?"

"Watch your backs, undie lovers." B.O. Boy blew a kiss and wheeled away on his bike.

The kids watched him go.

"Sheesh," said Zeke. He stank like fear.

Stephanie patted Zeke's arm. "Don't think

about him now."

"Yeah," said Hector. "We've got plenty of other stuff to worry about."

"Sure," said Zeke. "But the other stuff isn't getting ready to cream my face."

Just then, Caitlyn rejoined us. "Stay close, you little trolltags. If you cause any trouble, I'll zelch you deader than a pootblast on a space shuttle."

I didn't know what she said, but I knew what she meant.

Of course, human rules don't apply to cats. I found a corner away from the action and began grooming myself. Eternal vigilance is the price of looking *this* good.

I had just finished my shoulders and was working on a hind leg, when a familiar smell teased my nose. Bitter, sharp, but oh-so faint.

The scent led me back into the crowd. I wove among legs as people hurried here and there.

Other odors distracted me: flowery perfume, stale bread and cheese, rich loamy dirt, the faint whiff of dogs, a metallic tang.

But the bitter scent lurked beneath them.

What *was* it?

A deep voice boomed, "Quiet on ze set!" And the crowd fell silent.

"Cameras rolling?"

"Rolling, Mr. Von Breif!" a woman replied from her seat behind a machine.

"Und . . . *action!*" cried Von Breif.

A black box belched out mist. Five humans in silver suits ran onto the field. The woman pointed her machine at the humans, and everyone stared, like this was the opening of a sardine can or something equally important.

My attention wandered.

Caitlyn and the children stood with the rest of the people behind a rope barrier, watching the silver suits. I ambled their way, still sniffing the air.

"Hey," I said to Stephanie. "Do you smell that?"

"*Shh!*" said Caitlyn.

I wound around Stephanie's legs. "Seriously, I can't place the odor, and it's driving me batty."

Caitlyn bent down. "Will you zip it and lock it, fuzz ball?" she hissed.

Something threw us into shadow, and I looked up. Two people and another machine sat on a small platform at the end of a long metal arm. The arm lowered, and the platform sank a few feet.

Suddenly the bitter smell hit me stronger than ever.

A man in silver ran past us and joined the others on the field. "Where's the transmogrifier?" he said.

"But . . . we thought *you* had it," a tall blond woman replied.

Peering out from the human legs, I saw that the new man was short and thick, with a moon-shaped face.

Stephanie nudged Hector. "That guy," she whispered. "Remind you of anyone?"

Caitlyn elbowed her. "*Shh!*"

Then two things happened at once.

Zeke gave a start, and I finally recognized the familiar rotten-egg smell of . . .

"The UnderLord!" cried Zeke.

'iddle Bitty Kitty Spy

"Cut! Cut! Cut!" bellowed Von Breif. "Who said that?"

The onlookers turned on Zeke. Anger scent bubbled around us like fresh coffee. But the boy was unaware.

"That's him!" he cried, pointing at Moon Face. "It's the UnderLord, I'm positive!"

"You sure are!" Caitlyn pounced like a mama cat on a sparrow. "You're positively going to *get it*, runt!"

But Zeke had slipped under the rope and dashed onto the field.

"Grab him!" someone yelled.

Zeke headed straight for Moon Face. "You can't fool us! We're onto you!"

"Who, me?" The man took a step back. "Somebody stop that kid!"

Three workers converged on Zeke.

That rotten-egg stench drifted around me, now strong, now weak. Carefully I edged among the human legs, following my nose.

Von Breif boomed, "Settle down, everybody! Ve must get some verk done." His platform lowered to human height. "You! Little boy! Leave ze set, now."

I squinted up at him, but couldn't make out much against the lights' glare.

"No!" said Zeke, struggling between two men. "You've got a dangerous impostor working on your movie."

"Impostor?" said the director.

65

Moon Face spread his arms. "Of *course* I'm an impostor," he said. "I'm an *actor*. That's what acting is all about."

Some of the onlookers laughed. I slipped under the rope barrier.

"He's not an actor," said Zeke. "He's the Under-Lord, and he's trying to take over our world."

"Someone's been vatching too much TV." Von Breif chuckled. "Now, who is responsible for this boy?"

Caitlyn shuffled forward. "Um, me, if you want to get technical about it. But he's going to like, totally wish I wasn't, the little blivet."

"Young lady, take him avay. He is banned from this set, *ja?*"

Caitlyn grabbed Zeke's arm. "Oh, *ja*. Come along, Zekey boy."

I worked my way close to Moon Face and took a deep sniff. He reeked of pickle and hamburger,

of too much sweat and not enough flowery perfume.

But no rotten-egg smell—none at all.

I turned. "Hector, Stephanie!" I called. "This
guy's not the UnderLord."

"Und get that cat out of here!" Von Breif
boomed. "This is not a zoo."

A workman grabbed at me. I scampered out of
reach, back into the crowd.

"Hector?" I called, dodging through the forest
of legs.

"Here, Fitzie," he said. Hector squatted, and
when I trotted up, he scooped me into his arms.

"Don't worry," he said. "We wouldn't leave you
behind."

I twisted in his grasp. "Don't be a mouse brain.
I *want* to stay behind."

He followed Caitlyn and Zeke, and Stephanie
petted my head.

"You don't get it," I said, writhing until Hector stopped and put me down.

"Do you have to use the litter box?" he asked.

I rolled my eyes. *Humans.* Slowly and deliberately, I shook my head.

"Then what *do* you want?" asked Stephanie.

I looked back to the movie set.

"You want to stay?" said Hector.

I nodded.

From ahead, Caitlyn bellowed, "Get your meat buckets over here right now, bozinis! If Zeke has to go, everyone goes."

Stephanie's eyes widened. "You want to spy on the UnderLord?"

I nodded again.

"Good idea, Fitz," said my human. "Check it out, and we'll come get you tomorrow morning."

"Now means *now*," said Caitlyn. "Hel—lo? Am I like, speaking Norwegian?"

Stephanie and Hector hurried to join her.

I slinked back toward the action. Time for this panther to prowl. *Nobody* can be sneakier than a kitty on a mission.

Near one of the big metal boxes, I found a place to watch the scene and sniff the air. That rotten-egg odor still lingered. I'd find the evil little man that owned that stench, and when I did . . .

"Oooh, what a cute 'iddle kitty!" a bubbly voice cooed.

A female human descended on me in a cloud of jasmine scent. She was all smiles and curly red hair.

I gave her the big eyes and a little *"Mrrow?"* And before you know it, she was petting and fussing over me.

"Does 'oo want to stay here with me, 'iddle bitty kitty cat?" she said. "Mommy's got some treats, and 'oo'll be away from the big, bad director."

She carried me over to a cushy seat near the food table and laid out some sardines on a plate. "Comfy?" she asked.

To the untrained eye, it might have *looked* like I was being distracted. But as any kitty spy will tell you, it was just a clever way to infiltrate the enemy.

The crowd had left, and the workmen were shutting off the big lights. Jasmine Lady picked me up and cuddled me as she walked.

"Mommy's going to check in with the director," she said. "Then we can see about finding 'iddle kitty a nice, cozy-wozy sleepy spot. Would 'oo like that?"

I purred and closed my eyes. This undercover work was okay by me. Even if Jasmine Lady talked to me like I was a moron.

Up ahead, beside a big metal box on wheels, Von Breif was talking with three workmen. They were taller than he was, and they bent down like his servants.

". . . ready yet?" the director was asking.

"No, Mr. Von Breif," said a bony man. "It's complicated."

"I don't care!" boomed the deep-voiced Von Breif. "Ve must be ready in two nights, understand? Und I vant ze whole town here—everybody."

As we drew nearer, my cat sense kicked in. The hairs on my neck stood up, and I twisted in Jasmine Lady's arms.

"What's wong, 'iddle kitty?" she said. "Does 'oo want something?"

I growled, "Lady, if 'oo don't want a 'iddle bite, put me down. *Now!*"

Jasmine Lady's eyes widened, and she set me on the ground.

71

Away from her hypnotic petting and coddling, my mind cleared. Taking a deep breath, I caught the reek of rotten eggs, and I knew the truth at last:

Von Breif was the UnderLord.

And he was staring right at me.

CHAPTER 7

Fun with Fidos

Quick as a tail whisk, I shot under the big metal box. From the shadows I watched Rotten Egg Man.

"Vas that a cat?" asked the director. "I *hate* cats."

Not surprising, since I had bitten his butt the last time we'd met.

Jasmine Lady giggled. "Oh, um, yes, boss," she said. "But he's with me."

"Keep it *far* avay from me," he said.

"Yes, boss," said Jasmine Lady.

They chatted about costumes, and I kept my

eyes on Rotten Egg Man. What was this evil munchkin up to?

He dismissed Jasmine Lady, and she came looking for me.

"'Iddle kitty? Here, puss, puss, puss!"

I clung to the shadows under the huge box and kept quiet.

She moved off, calling, "Pussykins? Don't 'oo want some num-nums?"

A normal cat would've gone and had num-nums with the nice lady. But thanks to Rotten Egg Man and his magic, I wasn't a normal cat anymore.

I waited and watched.

Von Breif and the bony man climbed the steps of another big metal box. To the second worker, he said, "Turn them loose in five minutes."

"Sure thing, VB," said the man. He hurried off, calling, "Five minutes to lockdown, people! Five minutes!"

I waited until Von Breif closed the door and settled in with Bony Man. Then, a shadow among shadows, I slinked from my hiding place over to their box. The men's voices were muffled.

I crept up onto the steps.

My nose wrinkled as the stench of charred meat and foul cigars drifted from the box. Holy claw clippings! No wonder humans have such a weak sense of smell—your poor sniffers are over-loaded.

" . . . don't know what the big deal is," Bony Man was saying.

"Ze *big deal*?" boomed Rotten Egg Man. "Never you mind. Just build ze machine ze vay I've told you."

Their silhouettes showed against the window-shade—one tall, one short.

"But I don't see how it fits with our movie," said Bony Man.

"*You* don't see?" The short silhouette held up a coffee cup. "Who is ze director? Who is ze big man on set?"

"You are, VB."

"That's right!" Von Breif tossed the contents of his cup onto Bony Man—*sspissh!* "Und don't you forget it!"

The taller man seemed to shrink, lower and lower, to his boss's height. "Sorry, VB, sorry!" His voice piped, like a child's. "You're the boss."

My whiskers tingled. Something was fishy here, and not in a good, fishcakes-for-dinner kind of way. What was going on? I edged closer.

Okay, in hindsight, maybe I should've kept up my guard a little better. But that's what happens when cats act like humans.

A volley of barks broke my concentration. "*Rowf, rowf, rowf!*"

Fidos!

I whirled. Every hair on my back stood up.

A pack of huge, snarling dogs was galloping straight at me!

Fish bones and fur balls!

I leaped onto the railing and tried to scale the metal box.

Screeee! My claws slid down its side. The bird-blasted thing was solid metal.

I dropped back onto the stairs with a thump.

"Cat, cat! Bad cat!" the dogs bayed. They were almost upon me.

"Kitties ruuule!" I yowled, launching myself into space. I landed lightly on the lead dog's back, scampered across it, and jumped onto the next dog and the next.

They tried to turn and bite me, but the stupid Fidos were moving too fast.

Wham! They slammed into the stairs in a great heap.

"*Adios*, butt sniffers!" I cried.

I didn't wait for applause. I took off at a dead run.

Past the big metal boxes, past the empty food table I flew.

"Ground! Cat on ground!" The dogs clamored behind me.

I risked a glance back.

They were gaining fast. The lead Fido wore an especially mean look on his ugly muzzle; I didn't like the size of those yellow fangs.

A surprised workman stepped into my path. "Wha—?"

I dodged around him.

"Nice doggies?" he cried just before the pack swept into him.

A loud thump sounded behind me.

Eyes open wide, I scanned the night for shelter. A bush? Too flimsy. A cart? Too low.

Two trucks loomed ahead.

"Slow cat!" barked the lead dog. "Din-din."

Glancing over my shoulder, I flinched. He was only a few steps behind.

I zigged for the bush, then zagged for the cart. Yellow Fang was almost on top of me.

Fresh out of options, I ran right onto the cart. The dog followed, and his weight made it roll.

"*Woofa?*" he growled, planting his paws for balance.

The cart kept rolling toward the truck. Just a little farther . . .

Fimf! Light as kitten fur, I leaped from the cart onto the hood of the truck.

Whonk! The cart slammed into it. Yellow Fang tumbled.

Instantly the Fidos surrounded the truck, baying wildly.

I jumped up onto the roof of the truck, and

from there to the top of the high box behind it. Safe for the moment, I gazed down on the pack.

"Looking for someone?" I asked.

"Dead!" barked Yellow Fang. "Dead cat!"

The other dogs echoed his sentiments.

"The only dead thing I smell is your breath," I said. "Whooee, you stink."

And while they barked their fool heads off, I calmly gave myself a thorough tongue bath.

At times like this, it's sweet to be a cat.

The long night passed with many threats but little action. Growls and snarls were my lullaby.

When the morning came, two humans who smelled like coffee rounded up the dogs and dragged them away. When they were gone, I left my perch.

The film crew was stirring, preparing for another day's work. In all the hustle and bustle, I slipped through the gate and sauntered down the road.

The sun rose higher. I passed my time hunting birds. At last, Hector and his friends rolled up on their two-wheelers.

"Fitz!" called Hector. "*There* you are. I was worried about you!"

I trotted over to them. "Worry about yourself," I said. "I found the *real* Rotten Egg Man, and he's planning something."

Stephanie held up her hand. "Hang on. Before you get all *mrow-mrow-mrow* with us, just tell me: Did you learn anything last night?"

I nodded.

"Do we need to know about it soon?"

I hopped into her bicycle basket and nodded again.

"Then what are we waiting for?" said Zeke. "Underwhere, here we come!"